The Show Must Go On!

"What's the matter? Nancy asked Rebecca Ramirez.

Rebecca was almost in tears. "It's my talent show partner! She can't dance in the show!"

"Why not?" Bess asked.

"Her face is green!" Rebecca said. "Someone put trick soap in the washroom. After she washed her face, it turned green!"

"Do you want Nancy to find out who put the yucky soap there?" Bess asked.

Rebecca turned to Nancy. "I don't want you to solve a mystery. I want you to take my partner's place in the talent show."

Nancy stared at Rebecca. "Me?"

The Nancy Drew Notebooks

Available from MINSTREL Books

THE
NANCY DREW
NOTEBOOKS®

#33

The Gumdrop Ghost

CAROLYN KEENE
ILLUSTRATED BY JAN NAIMO JONES

A MINSTREL® BOOK

Published by POCKET BOOKS
New York   London   Toronto   Sydney   Singapore

This book is a work of fiction. Names, characters, places and incidents are products of the author's imagination or are used fictitiously. Any resemblance to actual events or locales or persons living or dead is entirely coincidental.

A MINSTREL PAPERBACK *Original*

A Minstrel Book published by
POCKET BOOKS, a division of Simon & Schuster Inc.
1230 Avenue of the Americas, New York, NY 10020

ISBN: 0-671-03709-9

First Minstrel Books printing October 1999

10 9 8 7 6 5 4 3 2

NANCY DREW, THE NANCY DREW NOTEBOOKS, A MINSTREL BOOK and colophon are registered trademarks of Simon & Schuster Inc.

Cover art by Joanie Schwarz

Printed in the U.S.A.

1

Ghost Grabbers
and Boo Blasters

If this is a theater, where's the popcorn?" Nancy Drew's best friend George Fayne asked on Saturday morning.

"This isn't a *movie* theater, George," eight-year-old Nancy Drew explained. "It's a theater for plays."

"And talent shows," Bess Marvin added. Bess was Nancy's other best friend. She was also George's cousin.

Nancy wiggled excitedly in her seat. The River Heights Kids' Talent Show would start any minute. Hannah Gruen, the Drews' housekeeper, had driven the girls

1

to the theater. She would pick them up when the show was over.

George's dark curls bounced as she looked around. "This theater sure beats our school auditorium," she said.

Nancy agreed. The theater looked like a palace. It had red velvet seats and clouds painted on a blue ceiling. A red curtain hung over the stage.

Bess sighed. "Maybe it's not too late to enter the talent show."

"Yes, it is," George said. "The show starts in five minutes!"

Nancy smiled. She and Bess had wanted to sing in the show. When Bess caught a cold the week before, they decided not to enter.

"Don't worry, Bess," Nancy said. "Watching the show will be fun, too. Especially since we have front row seats."

Bess reached under her seat and pulled out a white stuffed dog. "I'm going to ask the winner of the talent show to sign Sparky, my autograph hound."

"Even if the boys win?" George asked.

Bess scrunched up her face. Jason Hutchings, David Berger, and Mike Minelli were the brattiest boys at Carl Sandburg Elementary School.

"No way!" Bess said. "I hope that Katie wins. Or Rebecca."

Nancy flipped her reddish blond hair over her shoulder and smiled. "Me, too."

Katie Zaleski and Rebecca Ramirez were the girls' friends from school. Katie and her talking parrot, Lester, were going to tell jokes. Rebecca and her best friend, Jessie Shapiro, were doing a dance number.

Nancy gasped as the lights dimmed. The show was about to begin!

A man with white hair and wearing a dark suit stepped up to the microphone.

"Hello, everyone!" the man told the audience. "I'm Lyle Puckman, the host of the talent show and the president of Tremendous Toys."

Awesome! Nancy thought. Tremendous Toys was the biggest toy store in town.

"As you probably know," Lyle said, "the first-prize winner will receive a five-minute shopping spree at Tremendous Toys. And five minutes at Tremendous Toys goes a long, long way!"

Nancy knew which toy she would grab first—a pair of ice skates with pink pompoms. She had seen them when she was shopping for a present with her father.

"For our first act," Lyle said, "please welcome Jason, David, and Mike singing a song from one of their favorite TV shows, *Ghost Grabbers*."

"Oh, great," George groaned. "The boys are first."

"Now, remember, folks," Lyle said. "The boys' *Ghost Grabber* outfits, boo blasters, and spirit suckers are sold at Tremendous Toys. Aisle seven, shelf five."

Lyle walked off the stage. The boys ran on. They wore silver jackets, goggles, and helmets with blinking lights. Mike was holding a portable CD player.

Mike pressed a button on the CD player. The boys bumped into each other as they took their places on the stage. Then they began to sing.

"'If you've got a ghost—he's toast! Thanks to the Ghost Grabbers!'"

Nancy covered her ears. The boys were screaming into the microphone.

"'Ghosts are no mystery!'" the boys sang. "'They're *history!*'"

Jason raised his boo blaster in the air. It made a weird popping sound. Green gobs of foam oozed from the sides.

"Whoops!" Jason said.

The green gook flowed across the stage and onto the floor. It splattered right in front of the girls' feet.

"Yuck!" Nancy cried.

Lyle ran onto the stage. "You didn't tell me you'd have special effects!"

"I didn't press anything! It just went off!" Jason exclaimed. He banged his boo blaster on the stage. "Piece of junk. I'm taking this back to the store—"

Lyle clapped his hand over Jason's mouth. He called offstage: "Toni! Clean this up, please!"

A woman with short brown hair ran over with a mop. She was wearing jeans and a River Heights Theater T-shirt.

"I knew these kids would make a mess," Toni muttered.

Nancy watched Toni and frowned. She didn't seem very friendly.

After the floor was clean and dry, Lyle introduced the next act.

"Now here's Katie Zaleski and her fine-feathered friend, Lester!" Lyle said. "So 'give it up' as you kids like to say!"

"Yay!" Nancy cheered.

Katie walked onstage with Lester on her arm. She was wearing a red dress and a black top hat. Lester wore a tiny top hat and a little red bow tie.

"Knock, knock," Katie said to Lester.

Lester rolled his feathery head. "Who's there? Who's there?" he screeched.

"Boo!" Katie said.

"Boo hoo?" Lester squawked.

"Don't cry, Lester," Katie said with a wink. "You'll get your cracker."

7

Nancy laughed with the rest of the audience. Katie's jokes were always funny.

"Knock, knock," Katie said again.

"Arrrk! Who's there?"

"Orange," Katie said.

Lester let out a big squawk. "Orange you glad to see me? Arrrrk!"

Katie's mouth dropped open.

"Oh, no!" Nancy whispered. "Lester just said Katie's line."

Katie whispered something into Lester's ear. Then she tried again.

"Knock, knock," she said.

"It's Noah!" Lester squawked. "Noah good place to eat? Arrrk!"

"Th-th-thanks, everybody," Katie said quickly. Then she hurried off the stage.

"The jokes were still funny," Nancy said, shrugging. "Maybe she'll still win."

While the girls waited for the next act, Nancy felt Bess tug her arm.

"Here comes Rebecca," she said.

Nancy saw Rebecca running over. She

was wearing her talent show costume—a baseball uniform and a red cap. She also looked very upset.

"Please, Nancy," Rebecca said. Her chin was quivering. "You've got to help me! You've got to help me!"

2

Boo of a Clue

What's the matter, Rebecca?" Nancy asked.

Rebecca was almost in tears. "It's Jessie! She can't dance in the show!"

"Why not?" Bess asked.

"Her face is *green!*" Rebecca said.

"What?" Nancy cried.

"Did she eat too much pistachio ice cream?" George asked.

Rebecca shook her head. "Someone put trick soap in the washroom. After Jessie washed her face, it turned green!"

Nancy knew that Rebecca liked to be

dramatic. But she wasn't acting now. She was very upset.

"I'll bet the boys did it," George said. "They are such brats."

"Do you want Nancy to find out who put the yucky soap there?" Bess asked.

"If anyone can find out, it's Detective Drew!" George said proudly.

Nancy smiled. She loved solving mysteries more than anything. She even had a blue detective notebook where she wrote down all her suspects and clues.

Rebecca turned to Nancy. "I don't want you to solve a mystery. I want you to take Jessie's place in the show."

Nancy stared at Rebecca. "Me?"

Rebecca nodded. "You take dance lessons. And you're about the same size as Jessie. You can wear her costume."

"But I wouldn't know what to do," Nancy said. "I might look silly!"

"It's a cinch," Rebecca said, waving her hand. "Just watch me from the corner of your eye and do everything I do."

"Do it, Nancy," George urged.

"You might even win a shopping spree at Tremendous Toys," Bess said.

Nancy's eyes opened wide. She remembered the white ice skates with the pink pom-poms. She wanted them badly!

"Okay," Nancy blurted. "I'll do it."

Rebecca's tears disappeared like magic. She smiled and pulled Nancy out of her seat. "Let's go!" she said.

Nancy followed Rebecca backstage. Other kids dressed in costumes were rushing about. Katie was feeding Lester crackers. The boys were running in a circle around Jessie.

"Creature from outer space!" they shouted. "Green alien!"

"Go away!" Jessie snapped.

"Go away!" Jason mimicked. The boys laughed and ran to the water fountain.

"They're right," Jessie moaned when Nancy and Rebecca came over to her. "I do look like a creature from outer space."

"No, you don't," Rebecca said. "You look more like . . . a dill pickle."

"Thanks a lot!" Jessie groaned.

"Guess what?" Rebecca said. "Nancy is going to take your place. But you can still be in the act."

"How?" Jessie asked.

"You can start the CD player," Rebecca said with a smile.

"Yippy skippy," Jessie muttered.

"And if we win first prize," Nancy said, "I'll grab a toy just for you."

"That's more like it!" Jessie smiled.

Nancy and Jessie ran into the dressing room. They quickly exchanged clothes. When Nancy was in her costume she and Rebecca ran to the side of the stage.

"This part of the stage is called the wings," Rebecca whispered.

"Oh," Nancy whispered back. Rebecca loved the theater more than anything.

"Our next act," Lyle announced, "is Rebecca Ramirez and Nancy Drew, dancing to 'Take Me Out to the Ball Game.'"

Jessie flipped on the CD player. Nancy followed Rebecca onto the stage.

Nancy watched Rebecca from the corner

of her eye. She copied all of her dance steps. She kicked, hopped, and twirled her plastic baseball bat.

The audience cheered as Nancy and Rebecca took their bows.

"We were a hit!" Rebecca squealed as they ran backstage. "Tremendous Toys here we come!"

"I want the ice skates," Nancy said.

"I want the vanity mirror," Rebecca said. "To put on my stage makeup."

Nancy was still jumping up and down when she heard Lyle announce the next act.

"Now please give a warm welcome for Lizzie Benson!" he announced.

"Lizzie Benson?" Rebecca repeated.

Click-click! Click-click!

Nancy whirled around. A girl with bright red hair ran by. She was wearing a cowboy hat. Her cowboy boots had taps on them.

Nancy and Rebecca watched from the wings. Lizzie was standing in a spotlight.

"Howdy, everybody!" Lizzie shouted.

She waved her cowboy hat in the air and did a perfect split. "I'm Lizzie!"

Lizzie jumped up. She began to tap-dance. But she didn't just dance—Lizzie did somersaults, headstands, and cartwheels across the stage.

"Look at her go," Nancy whispered.

"Show-off!" Rebecca growled.

"Yee-haaa!" Lizzie shouted as she did a perfect back flip. Then her piano player handed her two sparklers. Lizzie held them in the air as she did one last split.

The audience went wild.

"We lost," Rebecca groaned.

Nancy watched Lizzie click by as she left the stage.

After more kids sang, did magic tricks, and told riddles, the show was over. Lyle called the contestants onto the stage. "Everyone deserves to win," he told the audience. "But since we have only two prizes, the first goes to . . ."

Nancy stood between Rebecca and Katie. She squeezed her eyes shut.

". . . Lizzie Benson!" Lyle said.

"Bummer!" Lester squawked. "Arrk!"

Nancy's heart sank. But she wasn't surprised. Lizzie *was* very good.

"Yippee!" Lizzie cheered. She smiled as Lyle handed her the certificate for the shopping spree.

"The second-prize winners will receive a fifteen-dollar Tremendous Toys gift certificate," Lyle explained. "And those lucky winners are . . . Rebecca Ramirez and Nancy Drew!"

"Ye-es!" Nancy cheered softly. She smiled as she took her prize from Lyle. But when she looked at Rebecca, Rebecca had a sad frown on her face.

"Now, don't forget," Lyle said. "There's a snack table in the back of the theater for the kids and their parents."

Nancy, Rebecca, and Katie walked backstage. They changed into their regular clothes, then headed toward the snack table.

"At least you won something," Katie said. "Lester and I lost big time."

"Losers! Losers!" Lester squawked.

"Guess what?" Bess said. She held up her stuffed dog. "While you were changing, Lizzie signed Sparky!"

Rebecca looked shocked. "You asked her for her autograph? Why?"

Bess brushed her blond bangs from her eyes. "Because she might be a star someday."

Rebecca gasped. "But *I'm* the best actress in school! Besides, if it weren't for Lizzie, Nancy and I would have won the shopping spree."

Nancy saw Lizzie at the snack table. She was pouring herself a cup of juice.

"I'm going to congratulate Lizzie," Nancy told her friends. She walked over to the table.

"Hi, Lizzie," Nancy said. "You were great."

"So were you," Lizzie said, smiling at Nancy.

Nancy noticed a gold charm hanging around Lizzie's neck. It was round with a flat bottom.

"That's so pretty," Nancy said. She pointed to the charm. "But what is it?"

"It's a gumdrop," Lizzie said. "You know, the gooey, chewy candy."

"I like gumdrops," Nancy said.

"I've got to go now," Lizzie said. She gave a little wave. "Bye."

Nancy watched Lizzie disappear into the crowd of kids.

"Well?" Rebecca asked Nancy when she returned. "Was she snooty? Did she brag about winning?"

"No," Nancy said. "She was nice. And she was wearing a gumdrop necklace."

"Gumdrop?" George asked. "You're making me hungry. Let's get some snacks."

Rebecca shook her head. "I have a better idea."

"What?" Katie asked.

"Let's explore the theater!" Rebecca said with an excited jump.

Nancy's eyes lit up. The theater was probably full of surprises.

"Do we have time?" Bess asked.

Nancy looked at her watch. "Hannah isn't picking us up for another hour."

"Then what are we waiting for?" Rebecca squealed. "Let's go!"

The girls ran toward the stage down a hallway on the side of the theater until Nancy found a door.

"Where does this door lead to?" Katie asked. She held Lester's cage in her hand.

"There's only one way to find out," Nancy smiled. She stepped through the door into another long hallway. A row of closed doors stood on each side.

"That one is open," Bess said, pointing.

Nancy looked where Bess was pointing. The door had a sign on it that read, Storage.

"Let's take a peek," Nancy said. She and her friends ran to the door. It creaked softly as Nancy opened it.

"Wow!" Nancy said as they stepped inside. The room looked like a secret attic.

Inside were a carousel horse, a table with a silver tea set, a lamp with a glass shade, and a rocking chair. There was even a pile of old hats, clothes, and a row of shoes.

"These things were probably used in plays!" Rebecca said excitedly. She pulled a feathered scarf from a hook and wrapped it around herself. "How do I look?"

"Like Lester." Katie giggled.

"Ha, ha," Rebecca said with a smirk.

Nancy saw a stack of colorful posters leaning against a wall. She began to flip through them one by one.

"Old show posters," Nancy declared. She held up a poster of a girl dancing. The girl had red hair and looked about eight years old.

"Who is she?" Katie asked.

"It says, 'Starring Miss Elizabeth Benson,'" Nancy said.

"I've heard of Elizabeth Benson," Katie said. "She was a kid star who grew up in River Heights. She died when she was very old."

"She *must* have been pretty old,"

George said. "The date of that show was practically seventy years ago."

Nancy studied the poster. "Benson . . . Isn't that Lizzie's last name?"

"And isn't Lizzie a nickname for Elizabeth?" Katie asked.

The girls stared at the poster.

"Her hair is red," Bess said. "Just like Lizzie's."

"And she tap-dances, too," George said. "Just like Lizzie."

Rebecca grabbed the poster from Nancy. She jabbed her finger at it. "So that explains it!" she said angrily.

Nancy turned around. "Explains what?"

Rebecca shook the poster in front of her. Then she exclaimed:

"Lizzie Benson is a ghost!"

3

Ghost? Or Toast?

A ghost?" Bess shrieked.

"Lizzie *can't* be a ghost," George said. "She was just tap-dancing an hour ago."

Katie shrugged. "Maybe she's a dancing ghost."

"Stop it!" Bess said. She clutched Sparky. "You're giving me goose bumps!"

"Don't worry, Bess," Nancy said. "There are no such things as ghosts."

"Oh, yeah?" a voice sneered.

Nancy spun around. Jason, David, and Mike were standing at the door. They were still wearing their silver jackets and blinking helmets.

"Why are you still wearing those goofy costumes?" George asked. "The show is over."

"The show may be over," David said. "But our job isn't!"

"What job?" Nancy asked.

The boys stood shoulder to shoulder. They pumped their ghost gadgets in the air.

"Ghost Grabbers!" they shouted.

Nancy rolled her eyes. The boys were always up to something.

"We're going to hunt down ghosts just like the guys on TV do," Jason explained.

David tipped back his helmet. "River Heights is crawling with ghosts."

"Give me a break!" George said.

"If you don't believe us," Jason said, "check out that creepy old house at Ten Tide Street."

David wiggled his fingers. "It's supposed to be . . . haunted."

Nancy knew the old house. It had peeling paint and broken shutters. The grass in the yard was long and dry.

"The house may be old," Nancy said. "But that doesn't mean it's haunted."

"That's what you think," Jason said. He reached into his pocket. "If you come across any ghosts, here's our card."

Rebecca took the card and frowned. "It's a baseball card."

"Our telephone numbers are on the back," Jason said. "Right under the batting average."

Nancy shook her head. "You're wasting your time. There is no such thing as—"

"Ghost Grabbers!" Jason shouted. He turned to his friends. "Forward march!"

The boys formed a line. Then they marched out of the room. "Ghosts are toast! Ghosts are toast!"

"I wish *they* were ghosts," George muttered. "Then they'd disappear."

Nancy saw Rebecca staring at the card. She had a dreamy look on her face. "My heroes!" Rebecca said.

"Heroes?" Katie cried.

"You mean *zeroes!*" George exclaimed.

Rebecca waved the card in the air. "We

need the Ghost Grabbers more than anything now," she said. "To prove that Lizzie is a ghost."

"Why would you want to prove that Lizzie is a ghost?" Nancy asked.

Rebecca smiled. "So she can be disqualified. Ghosts shouldn't be allowed in talent shows. They can do things that we can't."

Nancy shook her head. "Rebecca—"

"Think of it, Nancy," Rebecca said. "If Lizzie is disqualified, we'll win first prize—*and* the shopping spree!"

"But Lizzie is not a ghost!" Nancy insisted. "Everything on that poster is just a coincidence."

"Then prove it!" Rebecca said.

"What?" Nancy asked.

"You're a detective," Rebecca said. "And you probably brought your detective notebook with you, too."

Nancy could feel her blue detective notebook in her jacket pocket. It would be easy to prove that Lizzie wasn't a ghost. So why not?

"Okay, I'll do it," Nancy said. "Proving that Lizzie isn't a ghost will be a cinch. I'll start right now."

Nancy sat down in the old rocking chair. She pulled out her blue detective notebook and a small pencil. Turning to a clean page, Nancy wrote, "Lizzie Benson is Not a Ghost" on the top.

"I know," Nancy said. "I'll write down all the things that Lizzie did that ghosts *can't* do."

"Like what?" Rebecca asked.

"Like sign autographs," Bess said.

"Good, Bess," Nancy said. She wrote the word *autograph* on the page.

"What else?" Katie asked.

Nancy pressed her lips together as she thought. Then she snapped her fingers.

"Lizzie must live *somewhere*," Nancy said. "We can find out her address."

Katie reached into her small waist pouch. "I have a list of all the contestants and their addresses. I'll bet Lizzie's name is on it."

"Great!" Nancy smiled. She took the

list and read the list of names. "Michael Rossi . . . Sally McGarrity . . . Ben Soto . . . Lizzie Benson!"

"Where does she live?" Bess asked.

Nancy stared at the list and gulped. "She lives at . . . Ten Tide Street."

Bess let out a shriek. "You mean the haunted house?"

4

Calling All Ghosts!

Haunted house! Haunted house! Arrrk!" Lester squawked from his cage.

Katie placed Lester's cage on a small table. "Only a ghost would live *there!*"

"It must be a mistake," Nancy said. She pointed to the list. "And see? Lizzie wrote the name of her school. Ghosts don't go to school."

Rebecca looked at the list. "River Grammar School? Never heard of it."

Bess, George, and Katie shook their heads, too.

"Go ahead, Nancy," Rebecca said. "Write the haunted house in your book."

"But I'm supposed to prove that Lizzie is *not* a ghost," Nancy said.

"I have an idea, Nancy," Katie said. "Make a second page that says, 'Lizzie *Is* a Ghost.' Then, in the end, you can count which page has the most clues."

"Okay," Nancy said. She wrote "Lizzie Is a Ghost" on the next page. Then she wrote, "Ten Tide Street."

"But I'm sure this will be the only 'ghost' clue," Nancy added.

"You *are* going into the old house, aren't you, Nancy?" Rebecca asked.

The thought of the old house with the peeling paint made Nancy shudder. "I don't think so," she said.

Rebecca looked disappointed. "Detectives in the movies are always going into haunted houses. You're not scared, are you?"

"No!" Nancy insisted. "I just don't like . . . cobwebs!"

Katie grinned and raised her hand. "I have another idea."

"What?" the girls asked.

"The old house is the first ghost clue," Katie told Nancy.

"So?" Rebecca asked.

"So don't go into the house until you have three more ghost clues," Katie said.

Nancy thought a moment. "That sounds fair to me."

"It does not," Rebecca said. "The Tremendous Toys shopping spree is on Monday. You're just wasting time."

She took off her feathery scarf and threw it on the carousel horse. Then she headed for the door.

"Rebecca, wait!" Nancy called.

But it was too late. Rebecca stormed out and slammed the door.

"Don't worry, Nancy," George said. "Rebecca is just being an actress again."

"And you couldn't give me a million scrunchies to go into that creepy old house," Bess said.

"You already have a million scrunchies, Bess," George teased.

Nancy stared at her notebook. "I'll

never get three more ghost clues. Because Lizzie is not a ghost."

"What are you going to do, Nancy?" Bess asked.

"I wish I could talk to Lizzie," Nancy said. "Maybe find her phone number."

"Forget the phone number," Katie said. Her brown eyes were shining. "We can have a séance!"

"What's a séance?" George asked.

"It's where a bunch of people sit in a circle and talk to ghosts," Katie explained. "I saw it on that TV show *Creepy But True*."

"But Nancy is supposed to prove that Lizzie is *not* a ghost!" Bess argued.

"That's the whole idea." Katie grinned. "If Lizzie doesn't speak to us, then we'll know she isn't a ghost."

Nancy sighed. She didn't really want to have a séance. But it was better than going into the old house.

"Okay," Nancy said. She folded her arms across her chest. "But remember—I still don't believe in ghosts!"

George stared at the poster of Elizabeth Benson. "I think I do."

"So do I." Bess shuddered.

The door swung open. Toni, the woman who had mopped up the floor, marched in.

"What are you girls doing in here?" she demanded.

Nancy gulped. "Um . . . we're just . . ."

"We were looking for Lester," Katie blurted out. She pointed to Lester's cage. "There he is!"

"Arrk!"

"Hey!" Toni said. "I know that bird. He left cracker crumbs all over the floor backstage."

Lester blinked. "Ohhh, boy!"

"We were just going," Nancy said.

"What a meany," Bess whispered.

"What a meany!" Lester squawked loudly. "What a meany! Arrrk!"

"What did he say?" Toni demanded.

Nancy and her friends dashed out of the door and through the hall.

"I'll go home and get my room ready

34

for the séance," Katie said when they were outside. "It'll be soooo cool."

"Thanks, Katie," Nancy said. "We'll be there right after lunch."

Mrs. Zaleski picked up Katie and Lester. Then Hannah picked up Nancy and her friends. Bess and George were going to have lunch at Nancy's house.

"Pizza muffins," Nancy said happily as they sat at the kitchen table. "You're the best, Hannah."

Hannah smiled as she placed a platter of pizza muffins on the table. She had been the Drews' housekeeper since Nancy was only three years old.

"Don't mention it," Hannah said. "It's the least I can do for a real talent show winner—and her friends."

"Hannah?" Nancy asked as she reached for a pizza muffin. "Did you ever hear of a girl named Elizabeth Benson?"

Hannah looked up. "Sure. She sang this song called 'Gumdrop Garden.'"

Nancy almost dropped her pizza muffin.

She remembered the gumdrop charm around Lizzie's neck.

It's got to be another coincidence, Nancy thought. It's *got* to be!

The girls finished lunch. Then they walked the few blocks to Katie's house.

Katie was waiting for them on her doorstep. She was wearing a colorful scarf on her head and big hoop earrings.

"Welcome to my séance," Katie said. "I am Madame Zaleski! I am a medium!"

"No, you're not," Bess said. "You wear a size small, like me."

Katie looked annoyed. "No! A medium is someone who talks to ghosts."

Bess hugged Sparky. "Well, I hope they don't talk *back*."

Nancy, Bess, and George followed Katie up to her room. There was a round table set up in the middle of the floor. The curtains were closed, making the room very dark.

"Let's sit down and join hands," Katie instructed.

Bess tossed Sparky onto Katie's bed. Then the girls sat down and held hands.

"Now close your eyes and concentrate very hard," Katie said.

Nancy squeezed her eyes shut. After a few seconds, she opened one eye. She could see Katie swaying back and forth.

"Elizabeth! Elizabeth!" Katie called. "If you are in this room, give us a sign."

"What kind of sign?" George asked.

"Say hello," Katie suggested.

Nancy listened. The room was so quiet you could hear a pin drop.

"It's happening," George whispered. "The table is shaking!"

"Those are my hands," Bess said. "This is giving me the creeps!"

"Don't be scared Bess," Nancy said. "There are no ghosts in here."

"HEL-LO!"

Nancy jumped. The voice seemed to come out of nowhere.

"HEL-LO!"

The girls jumped up from the table and screamed. They bumped into one another as they tried to run from Katie's room.

"It's a ghost!" Katie cried.

The curtains began to flutter.

"Arrrk!"

Lester flew out from behind the curtains. He landed on Katie's head.

"Hel-lo!" Lester squawked. "Hel-lo!"

"It's Lester!" George cried.

Nancy was relieved. "You see? There are no ghosts in this room. Only parrots."

"Thank goodness!" Bess said. She fell back on Katie's bed. She picked up Sparky and gasped.

"What is it, Bess?" Nancy asked.

Bess held up her autograph hound. "Lizzie Benson's autograph! It's gone!"

5

Disappearing Act

What do you mean the autograph is gone?" Nancy asked. She ran over to Bess.

"Lizzie signed her name right under Sparky's ear," Bess said. She lifted the dog's floppy ear. "Now it's gone. See?"

Nancy looked at the dog. There was an empty spot where Lizzie's autograph had been. But then she saw some writing on the other side.

"Wait. There's something written under his *other* ear," Nancy said.

"What does it say?" Katie asked.

Nancy lifted the dog's ear and sighed. "Made in China."

The girls were silent.

"The autograph just disappeared," George finally said.

"It looks like a ghost clue to me," Bess said slowly.

"Two more to go," Katie said. "Then we go into the old house. Remember?"

Nancy shook her head. "There's got to be a reason the autograph disappeared. We have to look for more clues."

"Where?" George asked.

Nancy paced Katie's room. "I'd like to go back to the River Heights Theater. Maybe we can get permission to ride our bikes there tomorrow."

"I can't go," Katie said. "I have to take Lester to a birthday party."

George wrinkled her nose. "Parrots go to birthday parties?"

"Lester does," Katie said proudly. "His best friend is going to be ninety-nine years old!"

"Wow!" Nancy said. She knew that some parrots lived to be very old.

Nancy, Bess, and George said goodbye

to Katie and Lester. When they were outside, Nancy sat on a tree stump and wrote her new clue in her notebook.

"If Lizzie is a ghost," Bess said, "maybe she just wants to be our friend."

"She'd definitely be fun at sleepovers," George said.

"Why?" Nancy asked.

George grinned. "Think of the awesome ghost stories she'd tell!"

Nancy giggled as she closed her notebook. "I'd better go home now. I promised my dad I'd help rake leaves."

The three friends said goodbye. Then Nancy walked back home. She joined her dad in the yard and told him all about Lizzie Benson. Carson Drew was a busy lawyer, but he always had time to help Nancy with her detective cases.

"I thought you didn't believe in ghosts, Pudding Pie," Mr. Drew said.

"I don't, Daddy," Nancy said. She added some red and orange leaves to her pile. "But I keep finding clues that Lizzie might be a ghost."

Mr. Drew shook a few leaves off his rake. "Clues can be pretty tricky sometimes. That's why it's important to check out everything."

Nancy nodded. Then she remembered the sign-in sheet. "Daddy?" she asked. "Did you ever hear of River Grammar School?"

"Sure," Mr. Drew said. "It was an old elementary school. It was torn down about fifty years ago."

"Torn down?" Nancy gasped.

Mr. Drew nodded. "There's a parking lot where the school used to stand."

Nancy excused herself and ran up to her room. She sat on her bed and opened her detective notebook. Then she wrote the words *Old school* on the ghost page.

"One, two, three," Nancy counted out loud. "Three clues that say Lizzie *is* a ghost."

She fell back on her bed and groaned. "How can this be happening?"

*   *   *

Sunday morning Nancy, Bess, and George got permission to ride their bikes to the River Heights Theater. Nancy told her friends all about the old school on their way to Main Street.

"This is too weird, Nancy," George said as they parked their bikes outside the theater.

"I know," Nancy said. "But I'm going to get to the bottom of this right now!"

The girls walked up to the theater. Nancy saw a sign hanging outside. It said: *Snow White*. Show at 2:00 P.M.

"It's eleven o'clock now," Nancy said, looking at her watch. "We have plenty of time to look for clues."

Nancy tried to open the main door. It was locked. The girls ran around the side of the building. They saw another door with the word *Stage* written across it.

"Let's try that one," Nancy suggested. She ran to the stage door and twisted the doorknob.

"It's open," Nancy said. The girls slipped through. They walked down a short hallway that led straight to the stage.

"Neat!" Nancy said, looking around. The stage was filled with cardboard trees. There was a flat piece of scenery with a painting of a forest.

"It's Snow White's forest!" Bess exclaimed.

George pointed to the floor. "Looks like the seven dwarves were here. Check out the floor."

Nancy looked at the floor. It was covered with small dusty footprints.

"These footprints are probably from the talent show yesterday," she said.

Nancy got down on her knees. She began to crawl around.

"What are you doing, Nancy?" Bess asked.

"I'm looking for Lizzie's footprints," Nancy said. "She was wearing cowboy boots so her footprints would be very pointy."

George shrugged. "So?"

"If we find them, Lizzie can't be a

ghost," Nancy told her. "The ghosts in the movies never leave footprints. Their feet never touch the ground."

The girls got down on their hands and knees and searched through the foot-prints.

"I found it!" Nancy said. She pointed to a small pointy footprint. "See? There are no ghosts in this theater."

Bess tugged at Nancy's sleeve. "Um, Nancy? What happened to Snow White's pretty forest?" she asked.

"What do you mean?" Nancy asked. She glanced over her shoulder and gasped. The scenery was gone.

Suddenly the lights began to flicker. Then the stage began to move!

"Bess! George!" Nancy cried. "The stage—it's spinning!"

6

Dizzy for Lizzie

Lizzie is probably making the stage spin!" Bess cried. "She wants us to go home."

Nancy's heart was pounding. The stage wasn't spinning fast, but it was enough to make her dizzy.

The girls began to scream.

"Aaaaah!"

"Eeeeeek!"

Nancy saw Toni come running out of the wings. She stopped and flicked a switch on the wall. After a few more seconds, the twirling stage came to a stop.

"It stopped spinning!" Bess sighed.

"But my head didn't!" George said.

Toni folded her arms as the girls stood up. "You should not be playing on this stage. It could be very dangerous."

"Oh, we weren't playing," Bess said. "We were looking for a ghost."

"Bess!" George hissed.

Toni stared at the girls. Then she began to laugh. "A ghost?" she said. "You think this theater is haunted?"

Bess nodded. "Why else would all these weird things happen? The spinning stage, the flickering lights—"

Toni laughed. "A ghost didn't do that—I did."

"You?" Nancy asked.

"I was testing the equipment before the show," Toni explained. "That's my job."

Nancy smiled. So that explained the missing scenery and the turning stage!

"It must be fun working in a theater," Nancy said.

"Sure," Toni said, smiling. "When I'm not mopping ghost goo off the floor."

Nancy, Bess, and George giggled. Toni didn't seem mean anymore. She was nice!

Toni looked at her watch.

"How would you girls like a tour of the theater?" she asked. "You won't see any ghosts, but you will see how things work behind the scenes."

Nancy looked at Bess and George. They looked as excited as she was.

"Thanks, Toni," Nancy exclaimed. "That would be awesome!"

The three girls followed Toni around the theater. She showed them a special machine that lifted scenery right off the stage. There was even a whole room for all of the light switches.

If only Rebecca were here, Nancy thought. She would love this.

After Toni showed them the sound system, she let Nancy flip the switch on the side of the stage. The stage turned again. But this time they weren't on it.

"It spins so we can move sets from the back to the front," Toni explained. "It's a lot easier than lifting them."

When the tour was over, Toni led the girls to the main door. "Any more questions?"

"Just one," Nancy said. "Did you know Elizabeth Benson?"

"You mean the gumdrop girl?" Toni asked. "When she sang at this theater I wasn't born yet. But I did see her movie on TV."

Nancy was surprised. "Elizabeth Benson was in a movie?" she asked.

"It was called *Take a Bow*," Toni said. "It's probably in the video store."

A young man with blond hair ran over. "Toni!" he groaned. "Bad news. One of the seven dwarves is sick."

"Which one?" Toni asked.

"Sneezy," the man said.

"It figures." Toni sighed. She gave the girls a wave and ran off.

"I want to check out Elizabeth's video," Nancy said to Bess and George when they were outside. "Then we can see her up close and personal."

"My mom rents videos right here on

Main Street at Fabulous Flicks," Bess said. "I'll phone her to ask if she can bring her card."

Bess found some coins in her pocket. She used them to call her mother on a pay phone. In a few minutes, Mrs. Marvin drove up in her red minivan.

"Why don't you girls find your tape while I look around," Mrs. Marvin said as they entered the video store. "I want to rent a funny movie for tonight."

"Okay, Mom," Bess said. She turned to Nancy and George. "I hope Lizzie didn't make scary movies. I hate scary movies!"

Nancy saw a teenage boy standing behind a counter. He had brown spikey hair and freckles.

"Excuse me," Nancy said. "Do you have any Elizabeth Benson videos?"

"Elizabeth Benson?" the boy said slowly. "Isn't she the lady who does those exercise tapes? You know, *Steely Stomachs* and *Brawny Bellies?*"

"No," Nancy said. "She's—"

"I know!" the boy said. "She's that black belt karate star. The one who jumped out of the plane in *Chop-Chop Cop*."

"No! No! No!" George said. "Elizabeth Benson sang 'Gumdrop Garden.'"

"While she was battling aliens." The boy nodded. "In *Move Over, Martians*."

Mrs. Marvin walked over carrying a box. "Isn't this the tape you wanted, girls? It's called *Take a Bow*."

Nancy looked at the box. On it was a picture of Elizabeth in a garden.

"That's it," Nancy said. "Thanks, Mrs. Marvin."

The teenager took the tape box. He looked at it and shook his head. "She sure looks different without her ray gun."

Mrs. Marvin dropped off the girls and their bicycles at Nancy's house. The girls ran straight to the living room. After Nancy popped the video into the VCR, she pressed the Play button.

In a few seconds, Elizabeth Benson appeared on the screen.

"There she is!" Nancy cried.

The girls wiggled closer to the screen. Elizabeth was wearing a frilly dress. She was in a garden filled with lollipop flowers and peppermint trees.

"'Gumdrops growing in the sun,'" Elizabeth sang as she danced. "'Tasty, sweet, and lots of fun.'"

"Yuck," George said. "That's the corniest song I ever heard."

"But it's a great dress," Bess said.

A close-up of Elizabeth appeared on the screen. She had freckles just like Lizzie. And the same smile, too.

Nancy noticed something else. Elizabeth was wearing a charm around her neck. It was round with a flat bottom.

"Ohmygosh!" Nancy said, pressing the Pause button. "It's the gumdrop charm. Just like the one Lizzie was wearing!"

"Nancy," Bess said slowly, "that's another ghost clue. Does that mean . . . ?"

Nancy leaned back on her elbows and nodded. "We're going into the old house on Tide Street."

7

Knock, Knock. Boo's There!

Lucky Katie," George said as they rode their bikes to Tide Street. "She gets to go to a parrot birthday party."

"While we go into a haunted house," Bess complained. "And it isn't even Halloween!"

"Bess, George!" Nancy called from her bike. "We don't know if it's haunted yet."

But Nancy's heart was beating fast as they turned their bikes onto Tide Street.

Was Rebecca right? Nancy thought. Am I really scared?

The girls climbed off their bikes.

Nancy stared at the house. It had peeling paint and broken shutters.

"Let's not park far," George said. "Just in case we have to run for it."

"That does it," Bess cried. "I don't want to go inside!"

"That's okay, Bess," Nancy said. "You can wait out here in the yard."

The yard was filled with weeds and tall grass. An old broken swing hung from an old tree. It creaked back and forth.

"Um," Bess said. "I think I'll come inside. It's getting a little chilly."

Nancy, Bess, and George parked their bikes next to a row of trees. They walked to the house. The porch steps creaked as they walked up to the door.

Nancy held her breath. She grabbed the doorknob. The door made a creaky noise as she opened it.

Nancy, Bess, and George stepped into the entry hallway.

"Look!" George said. She pointed to the floor. "There's a piece of paper."

"Is it a note from the ghosts?" Bess said. "Are they telling us to scram?"

Nancy picked up the paper. "It's a menu from Angelo's Pizza Parlor."

George wrinkled her nose. "Ghosts eat pizza?"

The girls stepped farther into the house. A few cobwebs hung from the ceiling. The dusty windows made the house very dark.

Nancy reached into her pocket for her mini-flashlight. She flicked it on. The beam of light shined on a long staircase.

"Should we go upstairs?" George asked.

"No," Nancy said. "Let's explore this floor first."

The girls entered a room next to the staircase. Nancy shined her flashlight around. The room had dark wooden walls and a high ceiling.

"This is probably the living room," Nancy said.

George began to laugh.

"What's so funny?" Bess asked.

"Why would ghosts have a *living* room?" George said.

Nancy began to giggle, too—until she shined her flashlight against the wall.

"Bess! George!" Nancy said. She pointed to a portrait hanging over a dusty fireplace. "It's Elizabeth!"

Nancy stared at the portrait. It showed Elizabeth sitting in a green chair with pink roses. Around her neck was the golden gumdrop charm.

"It's that charm again," Nancy said.

"Gumdrops must have been her favorite candy," Bess said.

Nancy's sneakers squeaked as she moved closer to the portrait.

Why is the floor so sticky? Nancy wondered. She beamed her flashlight down. Then she gasped. Scattered on the floor were gumdrops.

"There's a trail of gumdrops on the floor!" Nancy cried.

"Ohmygosh!" George gasped. "Do you know what that means?"

"That Lizzie is messy?" Bess asked.

"No!" George cried. "Lizzie is *here!*"

Nancy stared at the gumdrops. She wanted to write the clue in her notebook, but her hands were shaking.

"L-l-let's go!" Nancy stammered.

The three friends turned and ran from the living room. But they didn't get far. A white sheet fluttered down from above. It covered the girls as they began to scream.

"Help!" Bess shouted.

"We're being attacked by a ghost!" George cried.

Nancy tried pulling the sheet off. Then she heard a familiar voice:

"Ghost Grabbers to the rescue!"

The boys! Nancy thought angrily. She tore at the sheet until it was off. Then she shined her flashlight toward the second floor landing. Looking down at them were Jason, David, and Mike.

"Aw, rats. We thought you were ghosts," Jason said.

Nancy stared at the boys. They were

wearing their Ghost Grabber uniforms again. "What are you doing here?"

"Rebecca Ramirez said there was a ghost in this house," Jason explained. "She asked us to find it."

David pointed to his stuffed backpack. "She even paid us—with candy."

"Candy?" Nancy asked.

David nodded. "All kinds. Chocolate, gummy worms, hot shots—"

Nancy put her hands on her hips. "Gumdrops?" she asked.

David reached into his backpack. He pulled out a jumbo box of colorful gumdrops. "How did you know?" he asked.

Nancy rolled her eyes. There were no ghosts in this house. Only pests!

"Come on, Bess, George." Nancy sighed. "Let's go."

"What's the matter?" Jason sneered. "Are you scared?"

George turned angrily to the boys. "We are not!" she said.

"You are, too!" David said. "You should have heard yourselves scream."

"We're not scared of any ghosts," David declared. "No way!"

Tap . . . tap . . . tap . . .

"W-w-what was that?" David stammered.

Tap . . . tap . . . tap . . .

"I don't know," Nancy said. She followed the noise down the hall.

"It sounds like it's coming from that room," Nancy said. She pointed to a room off the hall. The door was open.

"Maybe it's ghosts!" Mike whispered.

"Let's check it out," George said.

"You mean go in there?" Jason gasped.

"Sure!" George said. She narrowed her eyes. "You're not scared, are you?"

The boys looked at one another.

"Scared?" Jason scoffed.

"No way!" Mike exclaimed.

"Then come on," Nancy whispered.

The boys clutched their boo blasters and spirit suckers. The kids bumped into one another as they tried to peek through the door.

Nancy looked in first. The room was

empty except for an old piano. She could also see the back of a chair. It was green with pink roses.

It looks like the chair in Elizabeth's portrait, Nancy thought.

Then she noticed something else.

"The tapping is coming from behind that chair," Nancy whispered.

"Is not!" Jason said. "It's coming from behind the piano!"

Nancy shook her head. "It's—"

The chair whirled around. Nancy froze. Sitting in the chair was a girl with bright red hair.

"Hi!" the girl said as she tapped her foot on the floor. "Welcome to my house!"

8

"Come Fly With Me!"

It's Lizzie!" Nancy gasped.

"It's a ghost!" Jason shouted. The boys stepped back.

"Ahhhh!" they screamed. Then they turned around and ran out of the house.

"Some Ghost Grabbers!" George scoffed.

Lizzie stood up from the chair. She pointed at Nancy.

"Didn't you win second prize in the talent show?" Lizzie asked.

Bess and George clutched at Nancy.

"Sh-sh-she did!" Bess stammered. "But you deserved to win first prize."

"Thanks!" Lizzie said. She spread out her arms and ran around the room. "I can't wait to fly through that shopping spree."

"Fly?" Bess squeaked.

George gulped. "Like a g-g-g-"

"Hey," Lizzie said. She put her hands on her hips. "Why is everybody acting so loopy?"

"Because you're a ghost!" Bess blurted out.

George clapped her hand over Bess's mouth.

Lizzie's jaw dropped open. "A ghost?" she cried. "Who, me?"

"I can explain, Lizzie," Nancy said. She told Lizzie all about the poster, the gumdrop charm, and the Tide Street address.

Lizzie giggled. "Now it's my turn to explain," she said. "Elizabeth Benson was my grandmother."

Nancy stared. "Your grandmother?"

Lizzie twirled the gumdrop charm around her neck. "She gave me her favorite necklace when I was just five years old."

Nancy was still confused.

"But what about the school you wrote down on the contest list?" George asked. "It was torn down years ago."

"I know," Lizzie said. "I couldn't remember the name of my new school so I wrote down the school my grandmother went to. She always talked about it."

Nancy was still confused. "But what about your address?"

Bess looked around and made a face. "You don't live here . . . do you?"

"Not yet," Lizzie said. She did a few quick cartwheels around the room. "But after my mom and dad clean it up, we're moving in. I can't wait!"

Nancy heard footsteps in the hall. She turned and saw a man and woman carrying a mop, a broom, and a pail. They smiled at the girls and waved.

"I can't believe we thought you were a ghost, Lizzie," Bess said.

"And I can't believe I played another trick without knowing it," Lizzie said.

"Another trick?" Nancy asked, puzzled. "What do you mean?"

Lizzie's eyes lit up. "I love practical jokes! Squirting flowers, whoopee cushions, disappearing ink—"

"Disappearing ink?" Bess repeated. "So that explains the missing autograph!"

Lizzie nodded. "Wasn't that great? I wish I could have seen your face when it disappeared off your stuffed dog."

Nancy remembered another practical joke. "Lizzie?" she asked. "Did you also put the yucky green soap in the washroom?"

"Yeah!" Lizzie said, her eyes shining. "Was that cool or what?"

Nancy shook her head. "That was wrong, Lizzie. You ruined Rebecca's act. And you kept Jessie Shapiro from being in the talent show."

"Whoops," Lizzie said. She lowered her eyes. "I didn't mean to hurt anyone."

The girls were quiet for a few moments. Then Lizzie looked up and smiled.

"I have an idea," Lizzie said. She

looked at Nancy. "How would you and Rebecca like to run with me in the shopping spree tomorrow?"

Nancy couldn't believe her ears.

"I'd love to," Nancy gasped. "And I'm sure Rebecca would, too—but why us?"

"You did win second prize," Lizzie said. "And I'm supposed to bring two friends. I don't have any friends in River Heights yet."

"You do now!" Nancy said. "Thanks, Lizzie."

Bess began jumping up and down. "A Tremendous Toys shopping spree! Goody!"

Lizzie twirled her gold necklace. "You mean . . . goody *gumdrops!*"

The next day at school Nancy could hardly think about math, social studies, or spelling. Her mind was on the Tremendous Toys shopping spree.

As soon as school was over Hannah drove Nancy, Bess, George, and Rebecca to Tremendous Toys. Lizzie met them outside the store. She smiled and pointed to her red-and-white running shoes.

"This time I left my tap shoes at home," Lizzie said.

Inside the store Lyle Puckman led Nancy, Rebecca, and Lizzie to the starting line. Each girl got her own empty shopping cart.

Nancy glanced over her shoulder. A crowd of people stood behind her. Bess and George were holding Tremendous Toys balloons. Hannah was waving a sign that read You Go, Girls!

While the girls waited for the starting whistle, Nancy turned to Lizzie.

"I'm glad you're not a ghost, Lizzie," Nancy said.

"Me, too!" Rebecca said. "Now you can teach me how to do cartwheels."

"It's a deal," Lizzie promised.

Lyle held up his whistle.

"On your mark," Lyle shouted. "Get set—go!"

Lyle blew the whistle and the girls were off. Nancy raced up the first aisle.

She grabbed a doll for Bess, a soccer ball for George, and a mystery game for Jessie. Then Nancy grabbed the prize she wanted most of all—the white ice skates with the fluffy pink pom-poms.

A bell went off when the five minutes were up. Nancy, Rebecca, and Lizzie posed for a picture in the *River Heights News*. Then Lyle passed out cookies and punch to the kids. Nancy couldn't remember when she had had so much fun.

"When are you going to play with all of your tremendous toys?" Hannah asked later as she drove Nancy home.

Nancy sat in the backseat with her new ice skates on her lap. Her other games and toys were in the trunk.

"Real soon," Nancy said. "But first I have to do something very important."

Hannah glanced over her shoulder and winked. "I wonder what that could be."

Nancy smiled. She placed her ice skates on the seat next to her. Then she opened her notebook and began to write:

I still don't believe in ghosts.

But I do believe that anyone can be scared sometimes—even detectives!

I'm glad I went into the old house on Tide Street. Now I have a new friend *and* a new pair of ice skates.

And with all the mysteries I've been solving, I'll soon need a new detective notebook, too!

Case closed.

EASY TO READ—
FUN TO SOLVE!

THE
NANCY DREW
NOTEBOOKS®

JOIN NANCY AND HER BEST FRIENDS
AS THEY COLLECT CLUES
AND SOLVE MYSTERIES

IN THE NANCY DREW NOTEBOOKS®
STARTING WITH

#1 THE SLUMBER PARTY SECRET

#2 THE LOST LOCKET

#3 THE SECRET SANTA

#4 BAD DAY FOR BALLET

Look for a brand-new story every
other month wherever books are sold

Sabrina
The Teenage Witch™

Salem's Tails™

What's it like to be a powerful warlock,
sentenced to one hundred years in a
cat's body for trying to take over the world?

Ask Salem.

**Read all about Salem's magical
adventures in this series based on the hit
ABC-TV show!**

Look for a new title every other month

A MINSTREL® BOOK
Published by Pocket Books

EASY TO READ—FUN TO SOLVE!

**Meet up with suspense and mystery
in The Hardy Boys® are:**

THE CLUES™ BROTHERS
